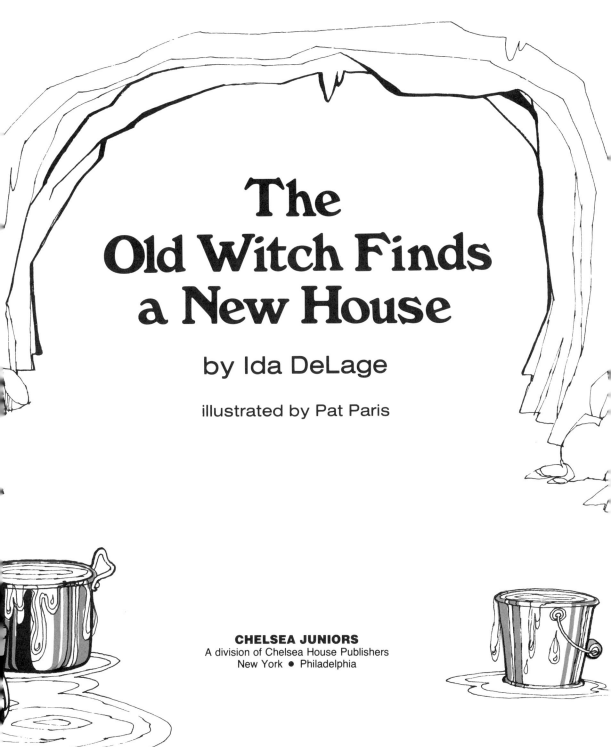

The
Old Witch Finds
a New House

by Ida DeLage

illustrated by Pat Paris

CHELSEA JUNIORS
A division of Chelsea House Publishers
New York ● Philadelphia

The Old Witch Finds a New House

A big cave
was in the side
of a hill.
The old witch of the hill
lived in it.

The old witch
liked her cave.
It was full of rats
and bats.
Sometimes spiders and toads
would come around.

The old witch would say,
"Come in, my pretties."
Then she would pop them
into her pot of witch's brew.

One day
the old witch said,
"I think I will go out
and fly around on my broom.
I will scare the chickens
and make them squawk.
The old farmer will think
a fox is in his hen house.
Hee-hee-hee!"
But when the old witch
peeked out of her cave,
what did she see?
Rain!
"Oh, fizzle!" said the witch.
The old witch didn't like
to get wet.

"I will stay inside
my nice dry cave," she said.
"I will cook my magic brew."
The fire was hot.
The witch stirred her pot.

Suddenly,
a drop of water fell
on the old witch's nose.
Then another drop came,
and another.
"Hmm-mm," said the witch.
"How can it be raining
inside my cave?"

The old witch looked up.
There was a little crack
in her cave!
Rain was dripping from it.
The crack got bigger
and bigger.
The drops came faster
and faster.

11

"Oh, fizzle-dizzle!"
said the witch.
"Where is my umbrella?"
But the water dripped
off her umbrella
and ran down her back.
It dripped into her pot.
It dripped into her fire.

The old witch chanted,

    "Drip drop, from the crack,

    go away and don't come back.

I hope my magic works,"

said the witch.

"Sometimes magic doesn't work on water."

But the drops kept coming.

The fire sizzled
and sputtered and smoked.
Then it went out.
"Now," said the witch,
"I can't make my magic brew."
So she hopped into her bed
and covered her head.
She took a long nap.

The old witch woke up.

She peeked out of her cave.

The sun was shining.

"Good!" said the witch.

She hopped on her broom.

"I am going out

to look for a new cave.

I have to move."

The old witch flew all over.
"I have to find a cave
with no cracks," she said.
She found two caves.
One was too small.
One had a bear in it.

The old witch kept on looking.

Just as she was flying over

the great, green forest,

she saw something.

"Look at that!" she said.

"Tree stumps!

A woodcutter must be around here."

Then the witch heard something.

Chop-chop.

Chop-chop.

There was the woodcutter.

He was chopping down
a big tree.

"Hee-hee-hee!"
said the witch.
"I will play a trick
on that woodcutter.
I will turn his ax
into rubber."

Just then,
the woodcutter yelled,
"TIMBER!"
The big tree fell.
But it fell the wrong way!
Swish!
The branches of the tree
fell on the woodcutter!
There he was,
stuck under the branches.
"Help!" yelled the woodcutter.
"Help! Help!"

Now . . .
the old witch played tricks
and she cast spells.
But she wasn't a mean old witch.
She knew she had to help
the poor woodcutter.
"I will put some magic brew
on the big tree,"
she said to herself.
"I will make it
as little as a twig."
But then she remembered
she didn't have any magic brew.
Everyone knows
a witch can't make spells
without magic brew.

"Great creeping lizards!"
cried the witch.
"Now what can I do?"
The witch flew down
and peeked into the branches.
The woodcutter was yelling,
"Help! Help!"

The old witch looked around.

Then she saw

the woodcutter's long rope.

"Ah ha!" said the witch.

"Just the thing!"

The witch tied the rope
to a branch of the tree.
Then she tied the other end
to her magic broom.

The old witch
hopped on her broom.
Up she flew,
over the trees.
Then, snap!
The broom stopped so fast
the witch almost fell off.

"Come on, old broom,"
said the witch.

"Fly, fly.

You can if you try."
The broom pulled and pulled.
It groaned and it creaked.
It pulled so hard on the rope,
it almost bent in half!

Then . . .
the tree moved!
Little by little,
inch by inch,
the magic broom
pulled the big tree up.
The woodcutter was free!
Quickly he wiggled out.

Suddenly,
there was a SNAP!
And a CRACK!
The magic broom pulled so hard
its handle broke in half!
Down fell the witch,
right into the branches
of a big tree.

The old witch hung
like an apple on the tree.
She kicked and she yelled.
''Help! Help!''
Now it was the woodcutter's turn
to save the old witch.
In no time at all,
he climbed up the branches.
He grabbed the old witch
and carried her down.
The witch picked up her broom.
She was very angry.
She jumped up and down.

"My broom!" she screeched.
"My poor old broom!
How can I fly?
How can I go out
and find a new cave?"
"Don't worry, old witch,"
said the woodcutter.

"I can make a new handle
for your old broom."
"Make it long," said the witch.
The woodcutter took his ax.
He cut a long branch.
Chop-chop.
He made a new handle.

Soon the witch's broom
was as good as new.
The witch hopped on it.
ZIP! Off she flew!
"I have to find
a new house," she said.

"She was a good old witch
to help me,"
said the woodcutter.
"I know what I can do
for her."

Chop-chop.

Soon the woodcutter had

a big pile of logs.

He put the logs

this way and that way.

"I will make a good house

for the old witch," he said.

The woodcutter worked hard.

He made four walls

and a roof.

He made a door to go in

and a window to look out.

He made a little chimney.

What a fine house it was!

The next day,
the old witch went out again.
"I hope I can find
a new home today," she said.
"I will fly over
to Big Rock Mountain.
Maybe I will find
a good cave there.
Oh ho!" cried the witch.
"What's that I see?"
Right in the middle
of the great, green forest
was a little house.
The old witch flew down.
"Oh, how lovely!" she said.
Then she read the sign.

The old witch
couldn't believe her eyes.
Her very own house!
"Eee-hee!" she said.
"Just what I need!
Maybe it will rain tonight.
I will move into my new house
right away," she said.

The old witch flew from her cave
to her new house,
back and forth,
back and forth,
all day.
She carried
her pot and her jugs
and all her other things.

At last

the witch was all moved.

She made a fire.

She began to cook her brew.

"What a fine house," she said.

That night,

the old witch went to bed.

The moon shone in her door.

The breeze blew in her window.

"How lovely," said the witch.

But then . . .
her candle blew out.
An owl sat on her roof
and SCREECHED.
Something BIG
looked in her door.
Something SMELLY
came in her window.

The witch didn't sleep a wink.
In the morning
the sun shone in her face.
A bird sang in her ear.
"That settles it!" she said.
The old witch knew
what she had to do.

"A witch needs a cave,"
said the old witch.
"I have to move
back to my old cave."
Back and forth
the witch flew all day.
She was moving her house!
The witch moved every log
of her new house
into her cave.
Then she put the logs
this way and that way.
She made four walls
and a roof with a chimney.
She made a door to go in
and a window to look out.

The old witch sat
in her new house-in-a-cave.
Her fire was burning.
Her magic brew was cooking.
"Maybe it will rain tonight,"
said the witch.
"How lovely!"